Stars out, moon out, too. Bedtime for you.

Up the stairs to run the taps on the bath. Bubbles. Boats.

Gloop - shloop.

igloobooks

Published in 2018
by Igloo Books Ltd, Cottage Farm, Sywell, NN6 0BJ
www.igloobooks.com

Copyright © 2018 Igloo Books Ltd

Written by Melanie Joyce
Illustrated by Gabi Murphy

Designed by Hannah George
Edited by Hannah Campling

GOL002 1018
2 4 6 8 10 9 7 5 3 1
ISBN 978-1-78670-298-2

Printed and manufactured in China

This igloo book belongs to:

....

Snuggle Up Tight

igloobooks

It's the end of the day.
No more play, toys away.

Rocket pyjamas,
nice and clean.

Brush your teeth
until they gleam.

Hop into bed.
Snuggle, cuddle.

Time for a story, the one
about the fairy? Nothing scary.

Sssh, settle down now.
Goodnight, sleep tight.

Click goes the light.

It's quiet and still.
Until...

... **Whooo! Tap-tap.**

What's that?
A cat, a bat?

Is someone outside? Quick, hide.

Don't look. Don't peek.
Try to go back to sleep.

Then, **turrrity-turr!**
There it is again.

Squeeze Ted tight. It's scary at night.
Squeeze Bunny, too.

Hoo-hoo!

Peek outside.

Eyes wide.

Who's there?

A tap. Then another.

Throw back the cover.

Rattle tap-tap on the window.

Time to go!

Run across the floor.

Dive for the door.

Race down the hall.
Teddy, Bunny and all.

Mummy, Daddy, there's a **monster** outside!

Mummy hugs, arms open wide.

There, there, let's go and see.
We'll find out what it could be.

It's not a monster,
just a tree, see?

Whooo!
goes the wind.

It blows the branches
to and fro.

So they
tap-tap-tap
on your window.

Hoo-hoo!

It's just an owl, in the night.

It's alright.
Click goes the light.

Soft and rosy.
Warm and cosy.

Back into bed.

Snuggle, cuddle. There are no monsters,
or scary sounds. No shadows moving around.

Time to snuggle up tight.

Goodnight.